THE SPECIAL DELIVERY

BY SAMUEL LANGLEY-SWAIN

ILLUSTRATED BY JEMMA BANKS

The Special Delivery (ISBN: 978-1-9997628-7-2)
First published in the UK, November 2018 by:
Owlet Press in collaboration with Festive Studio

Text copyright © Samuel Langley-Swain 2018
Illustrations copyright © Jemma Banks 2018

www.owletpress.com
www.festivestudio.co.uk

It was nearly time for Christmas and all through the school,
children were going crazy and teachers were losing their cool.

While their friends listed toys they'd hope to see in their sack,
Jack and Daisy invented thoughtful ways to give back.

Their neighbour, Pete the postman,
worked really hard throughout the year.
So, they helped him at his busiest time,
to deliver Christmas cheer.

They both made so much effort,
to tackle all his Christmas jobs.
By sorting cards, deliveries
and giving treats
to all the dogs!

"Where would I be without you?" smiled a very tired Pete.

"My helpful little Christmas elves. Time to rest our tired feet."

Just then, from inside Pete's van, came a gentle jingling sound.

They opened the doors, to find a chest with tiny fingerprints around.

At home both Jack and Daisy gathered everyone to see,
the many treats inside the chest, to make together, carefully.
There was a jar of magic snow, a plate for carrots and mince pies,
a Christmas drink and reindeer food. They couldn't believe their eyes!

So on Christmas Eve, the children
took the very greatest care;
spending time on every treat
their 'special visitors' would share.

"Sleep well, my little angels," said mum. "If you can't, try counting sheep!"
Both Jack and Daisy were ever so tired and drifting into a magical sleep.

Suddenly, from their window came a wonderful warming glow.
Jack and Daisy grabbed their wellies, running into the shimmering s[...]

They followed tiny footprints
down their garden path to see,
a tiny door, not there before,
at the foot of their tallest tree.

The children slowly opened the door
and were whisked straight out of sight...

They landed softly
at The North Pole,
amongst elves working
through the night.

"We know you've been so helpful,"
said one elf, "and making treats."
"Most children focus on getting toys
and eating lots of sweets."

"How do you know about us?" a very puzzled Daisy asked.
"Well, watching kids' behaviour is our other year-long task."

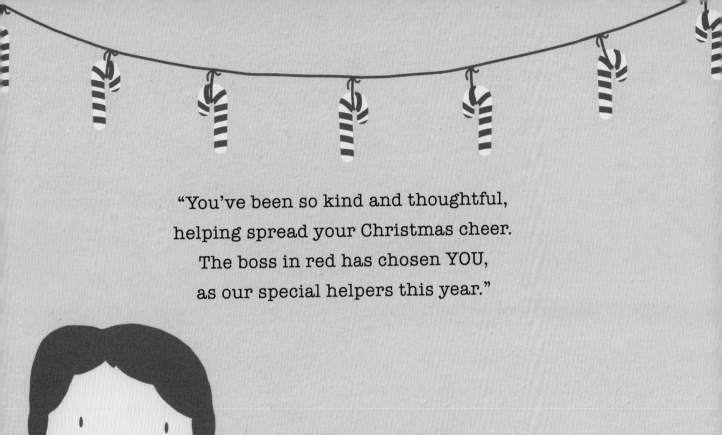

"You've been so kind and thoughtful,
helping spread your Christmas cheer.
The boss in red has chosen YOU,
as our special helpers this year."

"Can we help our neighbours first?" asked Jack,
"they've got no chimney you see."
"Don't worry Jack," the chief elf said,
"they'll have their magic key."

The children couldn't believe
this special task that they'd been given.
They spent the night sorting every gift
and curling every ribbon.

Jack and Daisy woke up stretching.
It was finally Christmas morning.
Had they REALLY been to the Elf Studio?
Or just dreaming? They thought, yawning.

They found sacks with their names on,
underneath the Christmas tree!
They carefully opened their presents,
showing each other their gifts with glee.

REINDEER
EXPRESS

FESTIVE DELIVERY SERVICE

TO BE OPENED BY:

Daisy

Official
North Pole Delivery

TO BE OPENED BY:

Jack

IF FOUND PLEASE RETURN TO:
THE NORTH POLE

DO NOT OPEN UNTIL
25TH DECEMBER

They'd hand-made presents for Grandma, one for Mum and one for Dad.
Hoping to make their family's Christmas the best one they'd ever had.

They remembered
what the elves had said
about their kind behaviour.

So they made a call
to Postman Pete,
to call in one last favour.

They dressed Pete's van with fairy lights
and tinsel like a sleigh.
A bright red nose on Rufus the dog,
made him like Rudolph, guiding the way!

They waved a Merry Christmas
to each neighbour at their door,

to make sure everyone loved Christmas,
just that little bit more.

At home that festive jingle came again at their front door.
Jack and Daisy thought it could've been a special delivery, once more.
Suddenly an envelope whooshed onto their front door mat.
"It's come from THE NORTH POLE," gasped Mum, "and golden. Fancy that!"

Official North Pole Document

Thank you Jack and Daisy.
You've been our greatest helpers yet.
You've given everyone a Christmas
that I'm sure they'll never forget!

The more love you put into Christmas,
the more joy you will get out.
You have shown
that being thoughtful,
is what it's really all about.

xxxxx

THE END